Highlights **Puzzle Readers**

LEVEL 2

LET'S READ, READ, READ

Knox Knocks
SPECIAL
DELIVERY

By Judy Katschke
Art by Josh Cleland

HIGHLIGHTS PRESS
Honesdale, Pennsylvania

Stories + Puzzles = Reading Success!

Dear Parents,

Highlights Puzzle Readers are an innovative approach to learning to read that combines puzzles and stories to build motivated, confident readers.

Developed in collaboration with reading experts, the stories and puzzles are seamlessly integrated so that readers are encouraged to read the story, solve the puzzles, and then read the story again. This helps increase vocabulary and reading fluency and creates a satisfying reading experience for any kind of learner. In addition, solving puzzles fosters important reading and learning skills such as:

- shape and letter recognition
- letter-sound relationships
- visual discrimination
- logic
- flexible thinking
- sequencing

With high-interest stories, humorous characters, and trademark puzzles, Highlights Puzzle Readers offer a winning combination for inspiring young learners to love reading.

This is Knox.

The K in Knox is a silent letter.

SNAIL MAIL

KNOX

He delivers mail—*snail mail*!
For a snail, *go* means *slow*.
But not for Knox.
He knows the best paths!

As you read the story, help Knox find his way through each maze.

The small box is for Cassie Cat.

CASSIE CAT

"I know a shortcut to Cassie's house," says Knox. "And it's a-mazing!"

Knox has a need for speed at Coaster Land.

Find the path to Cassie's house.

20

Happy reading!

Knox delivers mail almost every day.
Even on his birthday!

"I am too busy to celebrate," says Knox.
"My birthday will have to wait."

Knox has four boxes to deliver.
A square box. A tall box.
A red box. A small box.

Who will get snail mail today?

Follow the twisty stamp trails to find out which friend gets which box.

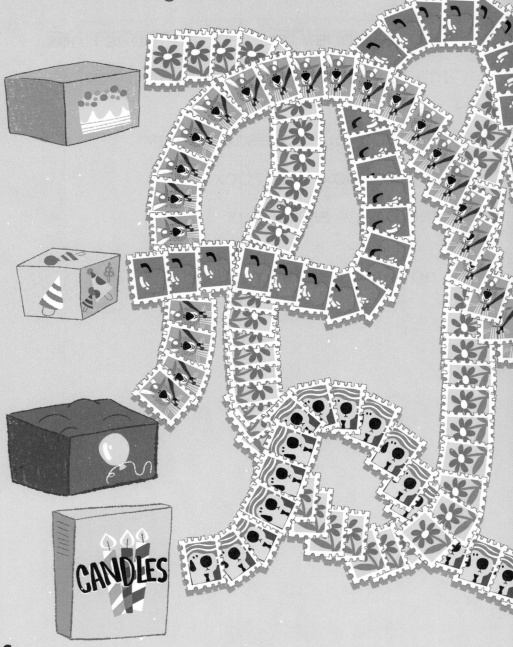

Rex Raccoon

Skye Firefly

Sammy Snake

Cassie Cat

The square box is for Sammy Snake.

"Getting to Sammy's house
is a piece of cake," says Knox.
"There's a shortcut
through the playground."

Find the path to Sammy's house.

START

FINISH

9

Knox reaches Sammy's house.

"Knock, knock!" calls Knox.

"Who's there?" asks Sammy.

"Bacon!" says Knox.

"Bacon who?" asks Sammy.

"Bacon this cake for you!" says Knox.

Sammy smiles.

Knox knows he's snailed it.
He delivered the first box and a smile!

The tall box is for Skye Firefly.

"I know a shortcut to Skye's house,"
says Knox. "It's through the dog park!"

Find the path to Skye's house.

START

FINISH

13

Knox knocks on Skye's door.

He delivers the box and a riddle.

"Why do fireflies love school?" asks Knox.

"Why?" asks Skye.

"Because they're so bright!" says Knox.

The red box is for Rex Raccoon.

"I know a shortcut to Rex's house," says Knox. "And it's sky-high."

Snail mail becomes air mail for Knox!

Find the path to Rex's house.

START

FINISH

17

Knox touches down at Rex's house.

"Knock, knock!" calls Knox.

"Who's there?" asks Rex.

"Tank!" says Knox.

"Tank who?" asks Rex.

"You're welcome!" says Knox.
"Enjoy your balloons!"

The small box is for Cassie Cat.

"I know a shortcut to Cassie's house,"
says Knox. "And it's a-mazing!"

Knox has a need for speed at Coaster Land.

Find the path to Cassie's house.

FINISH

START

21

Knox reaches Cassie's house.
He delivers the hats—and a riddle!

"What is a cat's favorite color?" asks Knox.

"I don't know," says Cassie.

"It's *purrrrrr*-ple," says Knox. "Just kitten!"

Knox is one happy snail.

He delivered all four boxes!

So why is his bag still heavy?

Knox flips his bag upside down.
Out falls a gray box with a PLUNK!

"I don't remember this box," says Knox.
"I wonder where it needs to go."

Knox reads the label:

"*Right away?* I better get going!"

says Knox.

Find the path to the park.

At the park, Knox sees the balloons.

He sees the candles on the cake.

He sees his friends wearing the hats.

"Surprise!" they shout.

Knox was so busy.

He forgot to celebrate his birthday.

But his friends did not!

Thanks to his friends,
Knox has the best birthday ever.
And when he opens the blue box,
he has the best birthday present.

Happy Birthday, Knox!

Knox's Favorite

Knock, knock.

Who's there?

Doughnut.

Doughnut who?

Doughnut open this until your birthday.

What do snails do on their birthdays?

They shell-ebrate!

Who did the fawn invite to her birthday party?

Her nearest and deer-est friends

Birthday Jokes

When do kangaroos celebrate their birthdays?

During leap year

What do bunnies sing at birthday parties?

Hoppy Birthday!

Knock, knock.

Who's there?

Hippo.

Hippo who?

Hippo birthday to you!